NEW HAVEN PUBLIC LIBRARY
3 5000 09409 1138

W9-DFG-674

Big Little Elephant

VALERI GORBACHEV

GULLIVER BOOKS * HARCOURT, INC.
Orlando Austin New York San Diego Toronto London

www.HarcourtBooks.com

Gulliver Books is a trademark of Harcourt, Inc., registered in the United States of America and/or other jurisdictions.

Library of Congress Cataloging-in-Publication Data
Gorbachev, Valeri.
Big Little Elephant/Valeri Gorbachev.
p. cm.
Summary: Little Elephant finally makes some friends, but he has trouble playing with them because of his size.
[1. Size—Fiction. 2. Friendship—Fiction. 3. Play—Fiction. 4. Elephants—Fiction.] I. Title.
PZ7.G6475Bgl 2005
[E]—dc22 2004017717
ISBN 0-15-205195-3
First edition
H G F E D C B A

Manufactured in China

The illustrations in this book were done in pen-and-ink and watercolors.
The display type was set in Sunshine.
The text type was set in Sunshine.
Color separations by Colourscan Co. Pte. Ltd., Singapore
Manufactured by South China Printing Company, Ltd., China
This book was printed on totally chlorine-free Stora Enso Matte paper.
Production supervision by Pascha Gerlinger
Designed by Linda Lockowitz

To my friend Ruben Varshamov

—V. G.

Little Elephant lived in a cozy house. He had lots of fun toys and books, and a caring mother and father. But Little Elephant had a big problem.

Little Elephant did not have any friends.

Little Elephant spent lots of time
dreaming about meeting a friend.

One day Little Elephant was out walking, alone as always. Suddenly, off in the distance, he saw a big group of small friends playing in the water. They looked very happy.

"Oh!" gasped Little Elephant. "Maybe I could play with them!"

"Hello!" he said. "I am Little Elephant. Can I play with you?"
"Sure," said Heron. "Come splash in the lake with us."
"It's lots of fun!" cried Green Frog and Yellow Frog.

"And after that, we could jump rope," said Heron.
"It's lots of fun!" cried Green Frog and Yellow Frog.
"Then we could play hopscotch," said Turtle.
"That's fun, too!" cried Green Frog and Yellow Frog.

"Okay!" said Little Elephant.
He jumped into the water and made a BIG splash.
"Stop! Stop! Stop!" cried Heron, Turtle, Green Frog, and Yellow Frog.

"I'm sorry," said Little Elephant. "Maybe I am not very good at splashing in the water. Could we jump rope instead?"

"Oh . . . we are not so sure," said Heron, Turtle, Green Frog, and Yellow Frog. "We can't move the rope, Little Elephant."

"I'm sorry," said Little Elephant. "I guess
I'm not very good at jumping rope, either.
How about hopscotch?"
"No! No!" cried Turtle, Frogs, and Heron.
"It's very scary when you balance on one leg,
Little Elephant," they said.

"You're too big, Little Elephant," said Heron. "We don't know how to play with you. We're sorry."

"I'm sorry, too."

Little Elephant went home feeling very sad.

"Why do you look so sad?" asked Mother and Father Elephant.
"I finally found friends," sniffed Little Elephant, "but I am too big to play with them."

"I can't balance on one leg like they do."

"I can't jump over the rope, and I can't jump into the water without making a flood."

"I'll never be able to do the things they do," cried Little Elephant. "I'll never have any friends at all."
"That's not true," said Mother and Father Elephant. "Maybe there are other things you could do with your new friends."
But Little Elephant didn't think so.

The next day Little Elephant went out walking, alone as usual. After a while, he came upon the same big group of small friends. But this time they did not look quite so happy.

"We can't fly our kite today, Little Elephant, because there is no wind," said Turtle.

"Well," said Little Elephant, "maybe I can fly your kite without wind."

And he did.
"Hurray!" cried Heron, Turtle, Green Frog, and Yellow Frog.
"You can do things that none of us can do," said Heron.
"It's great to have a big friend like you!"

"Really?" said Little Elephant.
"Really!" cried Heron, Turtle, Green Frog, and Yellow Frog.
"You're lots of fun!"

Little Elephant was still too big to do *some* things with his new friends.

But that was okay. They were all just the right sizes to do plenty of other things.

They were a very happy, very big group of big *and* small friends.